ROLE-PLAYING FOR FUN AND PROFIT™

BATTLE REENACTMENTS

MONIQUE VESCIA

rosen publishing's
rosen
central®
New York

With thanks to Matt Cleman, Civil War reenactor, who fights the good fight on and off the field.

Published in 2016 by The Rosen Publishing Group, Inc.
29 East 21st Street, New York, NY 10010

Library of Congress Cataloging-in-Publication Data

Vescia, Monique, author.
  Battle reenactments / Monique Vescia. — First edition.
     pages cm. — (Role-playing for fun and profit)
  Includes bibliographical references and index.
  ISBN 978-1-4994-3730-0 (library bound) — ISBN 978-1-4994-3728-7 (pbk.) — ISBN 978-1-4994-3729-4 (6-pack)
  1. Historical reenactments—United States—Juvenile literature. I. Title.
  E179.V44 2015
  973—dc23
                       2015021690

Manufactured in the United States of America

CONTENTS

Introduction 4

CHAPTER ONE

Battle Reenactments, Past and Present 6

CHAPTER TWO

Must Love History: How to Get Started 13

CHAPTER THREE

A Very Serious Hobby 21

CHAPTER FOUR

Making Money from "the Hobby" 29

CHAPTER FIVE

The Future of Battle Reenactments 36

Glossary 42
For More Information 44
For Further Reading 45
Bibliography 46
Index 47

INTRODUCTION

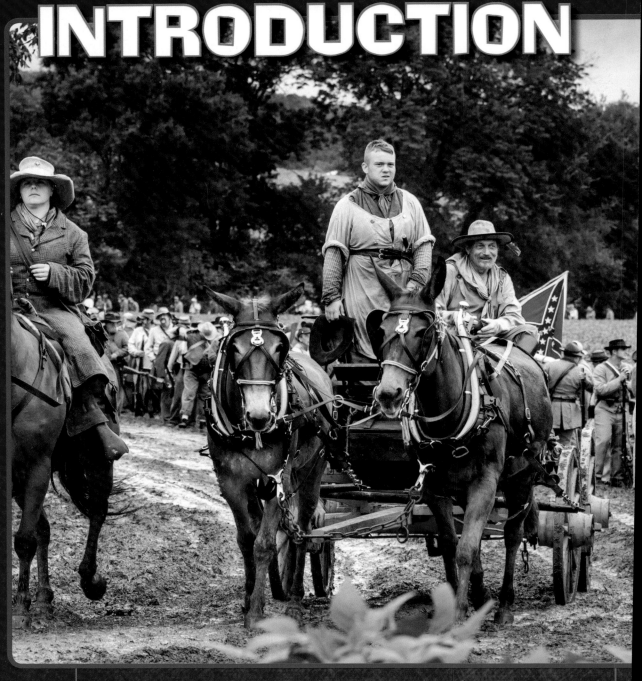

Reenactment events are often staged on important historical dates. Civil War reenactors outfitted as Confederate troops march in the Georgia mud during the 150th anniversary of the Battle of Chickamauga.

Some people say they were born in the wrong century, or even in the wrong millennium. History fascinates them, and they feel drawn to a time before electricity or cars or smartphones. They wonder what it would feel like to march into battle wearing a hand-stitched uniform and carrying a musket. They imagine themselves falling asleep on the rocky ground and waking up to the sound of a bugle.

People with a keen interest in military history can "relive" famous events of the past when they participate in historical reenactments. Battle reenactments strive to re-create the appearance, conditions, and experience of a historic armed conflict—without the casualties, of course. Reenactors wear period clothing and carry authentic-looking gear and weapons. They undergo the field conditions of an army when they camp in tents and build fires to keep warm and cook food. When the call to arms sounds, they take to the field and clash with "enemy" troops, sometimes on the same site where a famous battle was once fought—usually in front of crowds of spectators.

Becoming a battle reenactor requires time and money. Some reenactors earn money as film extras or as consultants on movie sets. Others give living history demonstrations. Most do it as a hobby, for fun and fellowship.

Judging by the number of groups dedicated to battle re-enactments in the United States alone, these time travelers are in good company. The largest community of U.S. reenactors depicts Civil War battles. Other groups restage conflicts from the Middle Ages and the Renaissance. Some reenact twentieth-century conflicts, such as key battles from the two world wars.

This hobby has ancient origins, and it continues to attract members and audiences in countries all around the world.

CHAPTER ONE

BATTLE REENACTMENTS, PAST AND PRESENT

One of the earliest forms of storytelling, battle reenactment has a long history. In ancient Rome, beginning in 80 CE, the Coliseum was flooded so that mock sea battles could be staged before thousands of thrilled spectators. Unfortunately for the combatants, these fights were usually to the death. Battle reenactments, sometimes re-creating scenes from ancient Roman and Greek history, became popular in seventeenth-century Europe. In 1638, a staged battle between Christian and Muslim forces delighted crowds in London.

The history of battle reenacting is probably as old as the history of warfare. Reenactments conveyed information about the fighting to civilians and celebrated the bravery of those who fought.

BATTLE REENACTMENTS, PAST AND PRESENT

Many people in the nineteenth century were fascinated by the Middle Ages. As they watched the world around them become more industrialized, they began to idealize the past. For them, the Middle Ages (500–1500 CE) represented a romantic time of highborn ladies and the chivalrous knights who championed them, of colorful tournaments and lavish castle banquets.

The largest battle reenactment of that century was the Eglinton Tournament of 1839. Held in Scotland, this re-creation of a medieval joust attracted 100,000 spectators. Due to pouring rain and bad planning, however, much of the grand spectacle occurred out of sight of the audience. Still, the Eglinton Tourna-

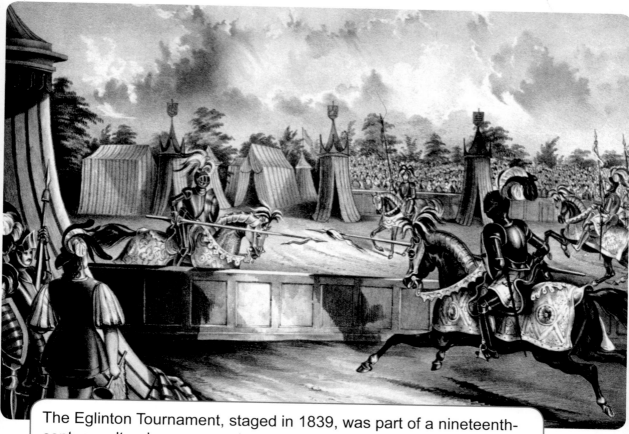

The Eglinton Tournament, staged in 1839, was part of a nineteenth-century cultural movement that romanticized the pageantry of the Middle Ages.

KNIGHTS IN SHINING ARMOR

If you've ever been startled by the sight of two knights in armor sword fighting in a local park, you may have seen members of the Society for Creative Anachronism (SCA) doing what they love. Founded in 1966, the SCA is the world's largest organization of Renaissance and medieval reenactment companies. More than 30,000 members of SCA meet all over the world to engage in tournaments and attend royal feasts, dances, classes, and workshops.

SCA members dress in clothing similar to that worn by Europeans before the year 1601 and practice the skills of the people of that time. They play ancient instruments such as lutes, weave cloth, and fire catapults. Members choose special names for themselves and reside in kingdoms of the "known world." The states of Washington and Oregon and the northern tip of Idaho comprise the Kingdom of An Tir.

ment inspired other medieval reenactments in Britain and the United States.

In America, popular homegrown reenactments included Buffalo Bill's Wild West. As part of the spectacle, reenactors restaged General George Armstrong Custer's 1876 crushing defeat at the Battle of the Little Bighorn, which had occurred less than a decade earlier. Some of the Lakota Sioux warriors who performed in the reenactment had taken part in the actual battle.

THE REVOLUTIONARY WAR

Battle reenactment is not simply a matter of dressing up in

authentic period clothing and pretend-fighting with replica weapons. Reenactment has always been symbolically important, a way of honoring moments of great sacrifice in a nation's history. Reenactors help tell stories about the past and educate people about its meaning.

No conflict was more essential to the formation and identity of the United States than the Revolutionary War. Between 1775 and 1783, many fierce battles were waged in the American war for independence. Revolutionary War, or "RevWar," reeenacting groups restage engagements such as the Battles of Lexington and Concord and the Battle of Bunker Hill, where American

Authentic-looking uniforms and replicas of historic weapons help American Revolutionary War reenactors create an "impression" of continental regular soldiers.

Patriots clashed with British soldiers and American Loyalists (those who supported the British king).

In March of each year, the Guilford Battleground Company restages the Battle of Guilford Courthouse. This hotly contested battle in 1781 succeeded in halting the British invasion of North Carolina. Afterward, Lt. Gen. Cornwallis, the defeated British commander, declared, "I never saw such fighting since God made me. The Americans fought like demons."

THE CIVIL WAR

In the United States, a majority of reenactors belong to hobby groups that stage battles from the American Civil War (1861–1865). Even before the fighting ended, veterans reenacted "sham battles"—clashes between Union and Confederate forces that honored their fallen comrades. These mock fights demonstrated to civilians what had happened in the war. They also helped keep the troops exercised and in fighting shape.

The Great Reunion of 1913 attracted 50,000 Civil War veterans from both sides of the conflict. The event culminated in a reenactment of Pickett's Charge, a climactic moment in the Battle of Gettysburg. The old soldiers met in fellowship on the same battlefield where fifty years earlier they had tried to kill one another.

American Civil War (ACW) reenactment is especially popular in Virginia and Tennessee, where most of the fighting took place. Interest in re-creating Civil War battles is not limited to U.S. participants, however. ACW hobby groups exist in many nations around the globe.

SPOTLIGHT ON GETTYSBURG

In a field in Pennsylvania now designated as the Gettysburg National Military Park, the granddaddy of Civil War reenactments takes place every year. The Battle of Gettysburg, which inspired President Lincoln's famous Gettysburg Address, was the bloodiest battle in the war. The three-day conflict in July 1863 resulted in 51,000 casualties (soldiers killed, wounded, captured, or missing). To this day, it remains the largest battle ever fought in North America.

In July 2013, to commemorate the 150th anniversary of the battle, between 60,000 and 80,000 spectators gathered to watch 10,000 to 12,000 reenactors re-create Pickett's Charge and other famous engagements of that momentous conflict.

OTHER CONFLICTS

Some hobby groups restage other battles fought during the nineteenth century, including the War of 1812 (1812–1815, between the United States and Great Britain) and the Mexican-American War (1846–1848). Conflicts popular in European reenactments include the Napoleonic Wars (1803–1815) and the Crimean War (1853–1856).

Beginning in the twentieth century, new technologies changed how wars were waged. Many reenacting clubs dedicate themselves to reenacting clashes from the First World War (1914–1918), once called "the war to end all wars," and the Second World War (1939–1945). A full-scale WWII reenactment may include troops, tanks, and historic planes roaring by overhead to give spectators a sense of the reality of full-scale combat. This century also witnessed the Spanish Civil War (1936–1939), the Korean War (1950–1953), and the Vietnam War (1954–1975), among others. Altogether, these wars made the twentieth century the bloodiest in human history.

CHAPTER TWO

MUST LOVE HISTORY: HOW TO GET STARTED

People with a genuine interest in a reenacting hobby should try to attend an event. Public reenactments are open to spectators. Many occur on the anniversaries of historic battles. Except for the annual Battle of Gettysburg reenactment, few take place on the actual sites where these battles occurred. Important battle sites have since become protected national parks, where reenactments are prohibited. Landowners and farmers sometimes rent out fields and wooded land to reenactment groups.

On a misty April morning in Virginia, spectators gather to witness a reenactment of the Battle of Appomattox, one of the last battles of the Civil War.

Serious spectators make the effort to travel to the places where reenactments are staged. Websites help people find events in their area. Those who can't make the trip can watch reenactment videos online.

Battle reenactments often appear as part of programs shown on the History Channel as well. However, there is no substitute for seeing a reenactment firsthand: hearing the shouted commands and the clash of swords on shields or the crack of muskets, and smelling the smoke and sweat.

FIND A MENTOR

As with any serious hobby, it helps to have a mentor—an experienced person who can share his or her experiences and expertise. Reenactors at events or demonstrations are there to interact with the public. They can answer questions and give you a realistic understanding of this hobby. Attend a Memorial Day parade. Reenactors often show up for these events and may have time to chat before the parade starts.

Reenactor groups all over the planet stay in

A reenactor describes troop movements during the Battle of Brooklyn. This important Revolutionary War battle was restaged in Greenwood Cemetery.

touch on the Internet. People blog about their experiences and exchange information. Those interested in the hobby can connect with other reenactors online. (As always, do not share any personal information, such as your full name, age, and contact information, with anyone you meet in cyberspace.)

JOIN A UNIT

In the United States, no single national organization of reenactors exists. Reenactors in each state belong to individual hobby clubs, which may be organized into larger umbrella groups. The smallest "unit" typically consists of a handful of people who reenact together. Larger groups may have elected officers, club dues, and regular meetings. These reenactors try to depict an entire military group, such as a regiment. Lists and contact information for reenacting groups can be found online.

Reenacting clubs are always looking for new members, or "recruits." Online magazines and newspapers for reenactors, which can be found at the back of this book, issue calls for new recruits. When reenacting clubs give demonstrations at battlefield parks, county fairs, and other venues, they often enlist new recruits on the spot. There is no age requirement for being a reenactor, but minors need a parent's approval and support.

Individual reenactors come from many different backgrounds. They may be lawyers, teachers, veterans of other wars, or even tango instructors. Sometimes entire families belong to clubs and participate at events. It's important that all members of a club work well and respectfully together. Do they have policies about women soldiers? Do they welcome members of the

AFRICAN AMERICAN CIVIL WAR REENACTORS

All-black companies, such as the 54th Massachusetts Volunteer Infantry (the subject of the 1989 movie *Glory*), fought heroically on the Union side during the Civil War. About twenty African American reenactment groups in the United States honor the sacrifices of black Civil War soldiers and bring their history to life. The African American Civil War Museum in Washington, D.C., is home to a group called FREED, or Female Reenactors of Distinction. Reenactors such as these women bring aspects of history to light that have too often been overwritten or ignored.

LGBT community? Some reenacting units allow Asian American recruits to play only Asian characters, such as in Korean War or Vietnam reenactments. African American reenactors may have limited opportunities in a Revolutionary War unit that depicts all-white soldiers. Potential recruits will want to determine if a particular club is a good fit for them.

Hobby clubs have uniforms and gear that they lend to new members. Reenactors joke that there are three sizes of Civil War uniforms: too big, too small, and doesn't fit. "Loaner gear" isn't always comfortable, but it allows new recruits to participate right away in reenactments.

CREATE AN IMPRESSION

An "impression" is a term reenactors use to describe the type of person or role they choose to portray. Clubs typically strive to present an impression of an entire unit or company of soldiers. New recruits begin as the lowest-ranking soldiers in that unit. Reenactors also present "civilian" impressions such as doctors and nurses, blacksmiths, laundresses, and other types present in military camps.

A successful impression is based on solid research. It's wise to avoid using films or television as a source for an impression, since costumes and props created for modern entertainment purposes may not be historically accurate. Instead, seek out primary sources such as diaries, letters, and photographs from the time. During the Civil War, many soldiers posed for a formal photograph before they marched off to war. The Library of Congress maintains an online archive of these images, which is a valuable resource.

The more a reenactor knows about the history of the period, the more convincing his or her impression will be. Spectators often approach reenactors with questions, such as: What are your religious beliefs? What are your feelings about the war? What did you eat for breakfast? Reenactors should be prepared to answer in character, as convincingly as possible.

ASSEMBLE A KIT

Assembling an authentic and complete kit is an investment. Depending on the specific impression a reenactor wants to create, the cost of a complete uniform, appropriate weapons, and related gear will usually cost upward of $1,000, and often twice that much. Authentic period costumes must be handcrafted, and weapons are expensive. Higher-rank uniforms and gear cost more, meaning a captain's uniform will cost more than a private's. Cavalry reenactors, who keep and outfit a horse as part of their impression, have even higher expenses.

People who sell period clothing and equipment are called sutlers. They often set up tents and display their wares at reenactments, in addition to selling online. New recruits should seek the advice of a veteran club member before making a purchase. Buying a used kit can save money. Check classified ads in reenactors' periodicals—retiring reenactors sometimes sell their kits.

FAR BE IT FROM AUTHENTIC

Authenticity is expensive, but most serious

A reenactor's kit includes a uniform, weapons, and related gear. The gray coat and blue pants signify that this uniform belongs to a Confederate soldier in the U.S. Civil War.

THE PRICE OF A SAMPLE KIT OF CIVIL WAR REENACTING GEAR

Trousers: $90
Shirt: $40
Sack coat: $90
Forage cap: $40
Brogans (shoes): $110
Wool socks: $11
Musket: $800
Bayonet and scabbard: $60
Belt, cartridge, and cap boxes:
    $95

Canteen: $50
Haversack: $30
Plate and utensils: $30
Tin cup: $20
Knapsack: $65
Wool blanket: $75
Gum (rubber) blanket: $85
Total: $1,691

reenactors try to avoid anything "farby" that will spoil the historical impression they want to create. In the reenactment world, "farby" or "farb" means anything, or anyone, inauthentic to a particular historic period. Wearing a wristwatch and drinking from a plastic water bottle at a reenactment is farby. Some clubs are more tolerant about inauthenticity than others. Reenactors who obsess about authenticity are known as "stitch counters."

Reenactors tend to fall into different categories. The majority are mainstream reenactors, meaning that they make an effort to look appropriate for the public. They may still wear modern underwear under period clothing, for example, or chow down an energy bar after the battle.

Progressive (sometimes called "hard-core") reenactors constantly strive to improve the authenticity of their impression.

This may mean soaking their brass uniform buttons in urine to achieve the right tarnished look, but that also means increased research and mental preparation.

READY, SET, REENACT!

Soon after joining a club, new recruits will have the opportunity to participate in a reenactment with their unit. First they need to learn how to drill, or how to march in military formation and use weapons in mock combat. Hobby clubs often use manuals written for the soldiers of that time period. Reenacting events for the public tend to focus on a specific battle. Most reenactments charge participants a small registration fee, though larger events may be more expensive.

CHAPTER THREE

A VERY SERIOUS HOBBY

After joining a unit, new recruits will have a chance to partici-pate in a reenactment and get a feel for how the unit works as a whole. As in a military group, new recruits can expect to be promoted as they prove themselves. In Civil War reenactment clubs, each new member begins as a private. Over time, members can rise to the rank of corporal then sergeant, followed by second and first lieutenant. The head of each unit, the captain, may be elected to that leadership position.

The soldier's equipment changes with each promotion. Those who are serious about the hobby will eventually want to assemble their own kits rather than continue to borrow loaner gear. Well-run clubs often have unit standards, which detail the proper uniforms and equipment that members should have.

A MORE AUTHENTIC IMPRESSION

Newbie reenactors often make the mistake of loading up on too much insignia. Insignia on a soldier's uniform identify rank. These

Reenacting is a physically demanding hobby. A reenactor must be fit enough to carry the heavy spear, shield, and armor of this Roman soldier under the hot sun.

may be embroidered badges on hats, shoulders straps, and special sleeve patches. But even when it dates from the correct period, all that insignia doesn't necessarily look authentic. The average soldier in the field was too busy trying to stay alive to bother with such things. As the Union general William Tecumseh Sherman said, "The longer the war goes on, the less our men look like soldiers and the more they look like common day laborers."

THE RISKS OF REENACTING

Reenacting is a very physical hobby and a dangerous one, too. Participants need to be in good physical shape. Uniforms may be made of wool, and military gear can be heavy. Many events take place during the summer, and some reenactors suffer from heat exhaustion. Accidents can happen in the most carefully staged combat.

The majority of reenactors who stage conflicts from the nineteenth century and later use real weapons, not replicas. They load their weapons with black powder, made from charcoal, saltpeter,

WHEN TO TAKE "A HIT"

How do battle reenactors decide who will "die" during a reenactment? Is it determined beforehand, or is it an individual decision made during the heat of the battle? The answer is complicated, but here are some reasons why reenactors choose to "take a hit" on the field:

- They run out of ammunition.
- Their weapons malfunction.
- They get bored. Yes, battles can actually be boring at times.
- They are tired, hot, or feeling ill. Wearing a wool coat and carrying heavy gear under the hot sun can lead to heat exhaustion. Sometimes reenactors get teased for crawling into the shade when they have been "wounded."
- An attacker "shoots" them at close range, or they are caught in simulated machine-gun fire. In other words, they should "die" when it seems clear they would have been killed in actual combat.
- There is a specific scene where casualties have been determined in advance. Sometimes the commanders will divide up the company by birth month, saying every soldier born in January and February will take a hit, and every one born in March and April will be wounded.

Soldiers who "die" on the battlefield have to resist the impulse to turn their heads and watch the rest of the battle play out. At the end of the reenactment, the order will sound across the field to "Resurrect!" and all the "dead" soldiers will rise to their feet again.

and sulfur, that creates clouds of foul smoke. At reenactments guns are loaded with blanks, like those used in the movies and TV. Blanks can still do serious injury, so reenactors generally don't allow the public to handle their weapons. Some reenactors purchase insurance to cover the cost of injuries. At some reenactments you must be insured to participate.

WOMEN WARRIORS

People in reenactment communities have strong opinions about the role of women in staged battles. Certain reenactment units

The reenacting hobby attracts women as well as men. Costumed as members of the U.S. military, these women participated in events held in France during the 70th anniversary of D-day.

don't allow "women in ranks," or WIR. They say that since U.S. women were not officially permitted in combat until 2013, they should not appear in reenactments of historic North American conflicts.

However, during the Civil War, at least 750 women (possibly many more) disguised themselves as men and fought alongside their brothers, husbands, and fathers. They served on both sides of the conflict. Some were so convincing that none of their fellow soldiers was the wiser. Medical exams were not very thorough—the army accepted anyone who could pull a trigger. Many young men who enlisted were too young to grow a beard, so a woman's lack of facial hair and higher voice might not give her away.

Some reenactors believe that if a woman can "pass" as a man, she should be allowed to fight. This might require wearing no makeup, speaking in a lower voice, and getting a short haircut. Some women reenactors flatten their chests with tight bindings. Kim Hofner, a reenactor and mother of two from Gettysburg, Pennsylvania, cross-dresses as a Union soldier to participate in the annual Gettysburg reenactment. Like many reenactors, Hofner believes she was born in the wrong time period. She feels very much at home in the year 1863, even though the authentic footwear makes her feet hurt. Women interested in joining a particular unit should find out what the policy is concerning female soldiers.

Public versus Private Events

One of the goals of battle reenactment is to educate the public and bring history to life. Some of these events are called "living history" and may attract large crowds of curious spectators. However, some reenactors also participate in private events, often called "tacticals." Tacticals are closed to the public and are sometimes labeled "EBUFU," meaning "events by us and for us." The people attending usually know one another. Participants must meet a high standard of authenticity—no farbs allowed! The events usually take place on private land, far out in the woods, with no bathrooms or running water or convenience stores located nearby.

Smoke from muskets drifts over the field as U.S. Navy, U.S. Marines, and militia men fire on British soldiers during a re-creation of a conflict from the War of 1812.

AN ENCOUNTER WITH THE PAST

Matt Cleman is a reenactor from Bend, Oregon. He belongs to two units and portrays both a Confederate and Union soldier at Civil War reenactment events. Matt first caught the reenacting bug during a family visit to Gettysburg when he was twelve years old. As he and his family picnicked at a table on the battlefield grounds, they heard rustling in some nearby bushes. Suddenly, two soldiers dressed in blue broke through the shrubs. Both groups stared at each other in surprise. "Don't you know there's a huge battle going on just over the hill?" one of the soldiers told them. "This is no place for civilians. I advise you to finish your meal and move on as quickly as you can." Then they turned and disappeared back through the bushes.

That encounter on the battlefield opened Matt's eyes to the reenacting hobby. Years later he told the story to some fellow reenactors as they all sat around the campfire at the end of a hard-fought day. One of them looked at him strangely and said, "You know, they don't have reenactors on the battlefield at Gettysburg." And Matt felt every hair on the back of his neck stand up.

TOTAL IMMERSION

Those who participate in tacticals tend to be progressive reenactors. They endure discomfort and hardship because they are seeking an experience of "total immersion." These groups wish to spend an extended time together immersed in the experience of being actual soldiers during a historic conflict. Some do not care for the term "reenactor" and instead prefer to be called "living historians" or "historical interpreters."

THE PERIOD RUSH

By paying strict attention to historical accuracy, hard-core reenactors hope to feel what they call the "period rush"—the sensation of traveling back in time to a specific moment in history. By wearing the same clothing, eating the same foods, and living under the same conditions that soldiers experienced in the past, these "progressive" reenactors chase that exhilarating sensation of what it was really like to be there. Many claim that by doing so, they pay tribute to the soldiers who actually fought in these battles.

CHAPTER FOUR

MAKING MONEY FROM "THE HOBBY"

For most reenactors, reenacting is purely a hobby. They enjoy getting together with other reenactors to pursue their shared interest in history. Some spend free time sewing period-appropriate garments, doing research, and refining their impression.

However, some lucky reenactors get paid to do what they love. They possess a wealth of knowledge and can lend their expertise to television and film producers. They may be hired to demonstrate historical weapons at a national park. Schools pay reenactors to give classroom presentations in

Glen Lawson, the commander of a Civil War reenactment unit, shows middle school students in Portland, Oregon, how to form a battle line.

character, speaking as a person from the past. History comes alive when students can ask a medieval knight what it feels like to wear 70 pounds (32 kilograms) of armor in the blazing sun, or question a red-coated soldier about British attitudes toward the colonists during the Revolutionary War.

Almost Famous

Some reenactors depict people who actually lived. Many individuals who do this feel like the characters chose them, rather than the other way around. In some cases, an individual may resemble a famous person from history.

Al Stone began portraying Confederate general Robert E. Lee after other reenactors kept mistaking him for the general at events. Stone, a Civil War buff, studied for five years before officially taking on this role. During his career he appeared as General Lee in more than twenty-nine movies. He gave lectures in uniform, speaking in character and revealing his deep knowledge of his subject.

Living History

Living history reenactment aims to teach about the past in a meaningful and more personal way. Living history museums and exhibits held at battlefield parks, county fairs, and other venues offer the public a chance to interact with people from an earlier time. Costumed actors answer, in character, questions from tourists as they enact scenes from daily life at a specific moment in history. Reenactors often volunteer at such events, but sometimes paid internships are available.

Reenactors can find paid full-time positions at historical sites such as Colonial Williamsburg in Virginia and Fort Henry in Ontario, Canada. They may demonstrate drills and battle tactics for the public. The National Museum of the Pacific War in Fred-

Visitors to Colonial Williamsburg, a living-history museum and tourist attraction in Virginia, watch as a professional reenactor incites his fellow colonists to resist British rule.

ricksburg, Texas, features a Pacific Combat Zone where battle reenactments take place. Hired reenactors bring World War Two to life. Visitors can feel like they are on the front lines, surrounded by the sights and sounds of a fierce battle between U.S. Marines and Japanese soldiers.

WORKING IN FILM

Dedicated reenactors have much to offer the film industry. In historical dramas that include battle scenes, hiring units of skilled reenactors can save film production companies money. Like a military group, a reenacting unit has learned to work well together. Members come equipped with period-appropriate

WAR AS A SPECTATOR SPORT: THE ETHICS OF BATTLE REENACTMENT

Some people feel that restaging battles glorifies the terrible business of war. They say the practice turns death into a spectator sport, a form of entertainment. In most cases, the National Park Service (NPS) officially prohibits reenactments on Park Service land. It claims that the black powder used in reenactments poses a danger (from lead exposure) to the public. Reenactments can cause damage to park resources and interfere with the memorial atmosphere of the site. However, the NPS does invite reenactors to give living history demonstrations in national parks to educate the public about important events.

Reenactors believe that what they do actively honors the memory of the soldiers who gave their lives in combat. In fact, many reenactors are veterans themselves. By replicating as closely as possible other soldiers' experiences, they can truly appreciate the extent of that sacrifice.

weapons, uniforms, and other types of equipment. They have experience depicting battle scenes and require far fewer takes than actors new to the roles do.

Casting services publish ads seeking reenactors for specific film productions. They post notices such as "Seeking: Soldiers, 18–40, Male, Caucasian. Thin to athletic builds required. Facial hair a plus but not necessary." They often ask reenactors to bring their own costumes and props to create a specific impression.

Joining a history casting organization can increase a reenactor's chances of finding film work. Reenactors may

Film productions often rely on reenactors to create authentic battle scenes. Director Christian Duguay prepares to shoot a battle scene for the movie *Joan of Arc.*

be hired as extras, stuntpeople, or actors. Extras generally appear in the background of a scene. The kinds of stunts a reenactor might be asked to perform include riding hard on horseback, fighting, and falling. Acting does not always involve saying lines but may involve close-up shots and specific reactions.

DON'T QUIT YOUR DAY JOB

Each type of on-screen work earns a different pay rate per day, but people do this for love, not for money. In some places, everyone participating in a film shoot, including the extras, must belong to a union such as the Screen Actors Guild (SAG). Reenactors can also earn money by loaning equipment such as rifles and cannons and sometimes animals (horses and livestock) to film production companies.

REENACTING ON THE SMALL SCREEN

Reenactors also have opportunities to work in television. They may appear in commercials or be featured in a TV series. The award-winning series *Canada: A People's History* relied on more than 200 reenactors to tell the history of that nation. Networks such as the History Channel air many programs and documentaries about specific events and periods in history.

Reenactment remains an important technique for depicting events that took place before the invention of photography and film. The people who produce shows for TV networks often hire reenactors to re-create authentic-looking battle scenes. Generally speaking, the smaller productions pay better rates—they don't have to hire as many people, so there is more money to go around.

CONSULTING

Individual reenactors may serve as consultants, helping film producers achieve more realistic effects in wardrobes and weapons, as well as in troop movements and the progress of filmed battle scenes.

As consultants, they might review scripts to ensure that the language used is historically accurate. The AMC series *TURN:*

CAMP FOLLOWERS

Civil War reenacting alone constitutes a multimillion-dollar industry. While the reenactors themselves may not be getting rich, plenty of people make money off the reenactment business, including:

- Sutlers
- Costumers
- Antique dealers
- Manufacturers of replica weapons
- Reenactment photographers and videographers
- Makeup artists
- Authors of reenactment manuals and history books
- Makers and sellers of commemorative merchandise
- Portable toilet suppliers

Washington's Spies could have benefited from a Revolutionary War reenactor's input. Characters in the series often use anachronisms such as "Yeah," "Okay," and "That's great," all expressions that didn't exist in eighteenth-century speech. A consultant also could have told the series' producers that the white wigs worn by the British characters were out of style during the revolution.

CHAPTER FIVE

THE FUTURE OF BATTLE REENACTMENTS

The majority of battle reenactment groups are based in the United States and the United Kingdom. However, reenactments attract participants and spectators in countries all over the world. Many reenactments commemorate major anniversaries of historic conflicts. Here is a sampling of events held around the globe:

Canada: The bicentennial of the War of 1812 drew record crowds of Canadians to witness lavish re-creations of battles that raged between Great Britain and the United States.

Czech Republic: Recently, more than two thousand participants took part in the Battle of Libusin. The annual event is a "fairy-tale" fight (not a commemoration of an actual battle) with reenactors depicting medieval knights from the ninth to the fifteenth centuries.

France: Second World War reenactments have become increasingly popular. Reenactments of the D-day invasion were held recently, seventy years after Allied forces stormed the beaches of Normandy, France, beginning on June 6, 1944.

British World War Two reenactors storm Gold Beach in Normandy, France, during one of many events staged in June 2014 to commemorate the anniversary of D-day.

Germany: Six thousand reenactors gathered to restage the Battle of Nations on the 200th anniversary of the date when a coalition of Austrian, Prussian, Russian, and Swedish forces succeeded in crushing Napoleon's army.

Israel: Recently, reenactors assembled in the Galilee region of northern Israel to restage the Battle of the Horns of Hattin, a decisive battle of the Crusades. The battle took place in 1187, when Muslims defeated Christian fighters.

Korea: Korean reenactors restaged an engagement in the Korean War (1950–1953) between opposing forces at the Battle of Naktong Bulge. To commemorate a conflict that Americans sometimes call "the Forgotten War," South Korean army soldiers dressed like North Korean soldiers to reenact this key battle.

The United Kingdom: More than four hundred reenactors traveled from around the world to participate in the annual reenactment of the Battle of Hastings, commemorating one of the most important events in British history. This gathering marked the 948th anniversary of the battle, when the invading French-Norman Army defeated the Anglo-Saxons in 1066. Armies of that time included archers, so reenactors with bows and arrows had to aim carefully to avoid hitting anyone.

BORDER CROSSINGS

Reenactors don't just restage armed conflicts in their own nation's history. The members of Nova Roma, which includes reenactors from all over the world, dress up like Roman legionaries, carry spears and shields, and re-create famous battles of ancient Rome. South American groups in Argentina, Brazil, and Chile present Viking impressions. The American Civil War is very popular with reenactors in Germany, Sweden, and Russia. Japan even has a large reenact-

Holding a battle standard that identifies his legion, a man dressed as an ancient Roman foot soldier takes part in a festival held annually in Lugo, Spain.

ment community that depicts Serbs, Croats, and U.N. peace-keepers and brings to life the fighting that occurred during the 1991 break-up of the former nation of Yugoslavia.

Some reenactors do not restrict themselves to a single historical period. They belong to multiple reenacting clubs and develop a variety of impressions, ranging from an eleventh-century Scandinavian housecarl to a fourteenth-century Mongol and a British officer in World War II.

LATEST TRENDS IN BATTLE REENACTMENT

Early reenactments often occurred very soon after the actual battles they were intended to honor. Today, the majority of reenactors re-create armed conflicts that took place hundreds—or even thousands—of years ago. Battles that happened in the distant past rarely stir up controversy. Enough time has passed that people have gained some perspective on the events. No veterans remain to challenge whatever account of the battle made it into the history books.

The idea of reenacting scenes from a war that happened mere decades ago makes some people uncomfortable. These conflicts seem too close in time, and the wounds are still fresh. Yet as early as the 1980s, reenacting groups began organizing private tacticals to restage battles that took place during the Vietnam War.

REENACTING VIETNAM

American responses to the Vietnam conflict (1954–1975) are

complicated. Many opposed the war—the second longest in history—and questioned the reasons for U.S. involvement in the fighting. Antiwar protests drew hundreds of thousands of demonstrators. Eventually, public opinion pressured President Nixon to begin withdrawing troops in 1970. Today, Vietnam stands as a cautionary example for military involvement abroad. In discussions of foreign policy, someone will often worry that a situation might become "another Vietnam."

The documentary *In Country* follows a contemporary group of Vietnam reenactors who re-create scenes from a jungle war in the woods of the northwestern United States. A number of these men fought in Iraq and Afghanistan. Sergeant Vinh Nguyen served in the Vietnamese army, fighting alongside American soldiers to oppose the Viet Cong, the communist forces trying to take over his country. For many of these former soldiers, reenacting functions as a type of therapy, a way of dealing with the trauma they experienced in combat.

THE FUTURE OF REENACTMENT

In Europe and the United Kingdom, 2015 was a busy year in the reenactment community. That marked the 200th anniversary of Napoleon's defeat at the Battle of Waterloo, and the 600th anniversary of the English victory at the Battle of Agincourt. As important historical dates come and go, reenactors expect to see fewer large events and a tapering off in their ranks.

Many reenactors are middle-aged, so hobby clubs are constantly on the hunt for new recruits. The allure of the past may not be equal to the appeal of the present, however. Some

REENACTMENT TV

Those who can't attend an actual reenactment might enjoy these programs:

- *Battle Castle* is a Canadian documentary series that uses CGI and reenactments to tell the story of six castles tested by siege.
- *Extreme Civil War Reenactors* follows a group of hardcore Civil War reenactors.
- *Weekend Warriors* is a comedy about the eccentric members of the British Civil War Society.

reenactors worry that potential recruits are more interested in ultra-realistic computer games such as Call of Duty, which create a virtual battle experience for the player. Or would-be reenactors may be content to "farb out" on the couch, watching reenactments, and shows about the making of reenactments, on television.

Since ancient days, battle reenactments have helped people come to terms with the past and reminded them of the terrible costs of war. That's a story that will need to be retold, again and again, until human beings finally find better ways of settling their differences.

GLOSSARY

anachronism A person or thing that is chronologically out of place. In modern warfare, a sword is an anachronism.

civilian A person who presents a nonmilitary impression during a reenactment, such as a doctor or a cook.

EBUFU "Events by us and for us"; acronym used to define private reenacting events.

farby, farb Reenactment terms meaning something or someone that is not authentic to the period. Serious reenactors consider it a terrible insult to be called a "farb." There are various opinions about the term's origin, but many say it is short for "far be it from authentic." Others claim it stands for "fast and researchless buying," a reference to the tendency of some newbie reenactors to purchase a lot of unnecessary gear.

the hobby Reenactors' name for what they do.

impression The persona of someone living during a specific historical period that has been created and presented by the reenactor.

insignia A set of symbols on a military uniform indicating rank.

living history An interactive presentation that uses historical costumes, tools, and activities to give participants a sense of stepping back in time.

mainstream A category of reenactor on the spectrum between farb and progressive. Mainstream reenactors make an effort to appear authentic in front of an audience but may step out of character when the crowds leave. Their uniforms may look handmade on the surface, but hidden finishings may be machine-sewn.

period rush The moment when a reenactor experiences the sensation of having traveled back in time.

progressive A category of reeanactor who is always working to improve the authenticity of an impression. Sometimes called a "hard-core" reenactor.

reenactor A person who participates in reenactments of historic events.

RevWar Reenactor nickname for the American Revolutionary War.

sham battle, sham fight Pre–Civil War name for battle reenactment.

stitch counter A reenactor obsessed with authenticity. Also called a thread counter.

sutler Originally, a person who sold provisions to soldiers. Today the term means a merchant who sells period clothing and supplies to reenactors. Reenactment events usually include a sutlers' row.

tactical Smaller private event held by reenactors for their own enjoyment. Authenticity standards are usually higher and conditions are rougher.

unit standards Specific rules regarding dress and behavior that all members of a reenacting club or unit are expected to follow.

FOR MORE INFORMATION

The Association for Living History, Farm and Agricultural Museums (ALHFAM)
8774 Route 45 NW
North Bloomfield, OH 44450
(440) 685-4410
Website: http://www.alhfam.org
This international organization is dedicated to making history relevant to contemporary lives.

Military Re-Enactment Society of Canada
16715-12 Yonge Street
Newmarket, ON L3X 1X4, Canada
Website: http://www.imuc.org
Members of the society present the Incorporated Militia of Upper Canada during the War of 1812. They drill regularly at Historic Fort York in Toronto.

The Society for Creative Anachronism
P.O. Box 360789
Milpitas, CA 95036-0789
(800) 789-7486
Website: http://www.sca.org
This is an international organization with over thirty thousand members dedicated to researching and re-creating the arts and skills of pre-seventeenth-century Europe.

WEBSITES

Because of the changing nature of Internet links, Rosen Publishing has developed an online list of websites related to the subject of this book. This site is updated regularly. Please use this link to access the list:

http://www.rosenlinks.com/RPFP/Battle

FOR FURTHER READING

Cornioley, Pearl Witherington. *Code Name Pauline: Memoir of a World War II Special Agent*. Chicago, IL: Chicago Review Press, 2013.

DK Publishing. *Military History: The Definitive Visual Guide to the Objects of Warfare*. New York, NY: DK, 2012.

Dougherty, Martin. *Medieval Warrior: Weapons, Technology, and Fighting Techniques AD 1000–1500*. Guilford, CT: Lyons Press, 2011.

Elson, Mark. *Battlefields of Honor: American Civil War Reenactments*. Oxfordshire, England: Merrell Publishers, 2012.

Forrest, Glen C. *The Illustrated Timeline of Military History*. New York, NY: Rosen Publishing, 2013.

Guntzelman, John. *The Civil War in Color: A Photographic Reenactment of the War Between the States*. New York, NY: Sterling, 2012.

Hambucken, Denis. *Soldier of the American Revolution: A Visual Reference*. Woodstock, VT: Countryman Press, 2011.

Hyslop, Stephen. *Eyewitness to World War II*. Washington, DC: National Geographic, 2012.

Kiley, Kevin F. *An Illustrated Encyclopedia of Uniforms of the Roman World*. Leicester, England: Lorenz Books, 2013.

Moss, Marissa. *A Soldier's Secret: The Incredible True Story of Sarah Edmonds, a Civil War Hero*. New York, NY: Harry N. Abrams, 2014.

North, Jonathan. *An Illustrated Encyclopedia of Uniforms of World War I*. Leicester, England: Lorenz Books, 2011.

Overy, Richard. *A History of War in 100 Battles*. New York, NY: Oxford University Press, 2014.

Schroeder, Charlie. *Man of War: My Adventures in the World of Historical Reenactment*. New York, NY: Penguin Publishing Group, 2013.

Watson, William J. *The Little Book of Civil War Reenacting*. Stroudsburg, PA: Broken Lance Enterprises, 2011.

BIBLIOGRAPHY

Braisted, Todd W. "TURN to a Historian." May 10, 2015. Retrieved May 10, 2015 (https://spycurious.wordpress.com).

Cleman, Matt. Interview with the author, May 12, 2015.

Fields-White, Monée. "Black Civil War Reenactors Reclaim History." The Root. May 5, 2011. Retrieved May 9, 2015 (http://www.theroot.com/articles/politics/2011/05/black_civil_war_reenactors_who_are_they.2.html).

Giles, Howard. "A Brief History of Reenactment." EventPlan. February 22, 2015. Retrieved May 3, 2015 (http://www.eventplan.co.uk/page29.html).

Horwitz, Tony. *Confederates in the Attic*. New York, NY: Vintage Books, 1998.

Miller, John. "How to Be a Reenactor." Emmitsburg Area Historical Society. Retrieved May 6, 2015 (http://www.emmitsburg.net/archive_list/articles/misc/reenactor.htm).

Mueller, Tom. "Secrets of the Coliseum." *Smithsonian*, January 2011. Retrieved May 3, 2015 (http://www.smithsonianmag.com).

Righthand, Jess. "The Women Who Fought in the Civil War." *Smithsonian*, April 7, 2011. Retrieved May 14, 2015 (http://www.smithsonianmag.com).

Schons, Mary. "The Past in the Present: Reenactors Bring American Civil War to Life." *National Geographic*. Retrieved May 5, 2015 (http://education.nationalgeographic.com).

Schroeder, Charlie. *Man of War: My Adventures in the World of Historical Reenactment*. New York, NY: Hudson Street Press, 2012.

Taylor, Alan. "Reenacting the Past." *Atlantic*, July 7, 2014. Retrieved May 1, 2015 (http://www.theatlantic.com).

Thompson, Jenny. *War Games: Inside the World of Twentieth-Century War Reenactors*. Washington, DC: Smithsonian Institution, 2014.

INDEX

A

African American reenactment
    groups, 16
authenticity, maintaining, 18–20

B

battle reenactments, history of, 6, 8

C

Civil War, 5, 10, 11, 12, 16, 17, 19,
    21, 25, 27, 30, 35, 38, 41
consulting, 34–35

E

ethics, 32

F

Female Reenactors of Distinction, 16
films, 5, 16, 24, 30, 31–33

G

Gettysburg, 10, 11, 13, 25, 27

H

hits, when to take them, 23

I

impression, determining your,
    16–17

L

living history, 5, 30–31, 32

M

mentors, 14–15

P

private versus public events, 25–26

R

reenacting
    assembling and buying gear,
        17–18, 19
    careers in, 28–35
    dangers of, 22–24
    employees in the business, 35
    firsthand account of, 27
    and women, 16, 24–25
Revolutionary War, 9–10, 16, 30, 35

S

Society for Creative Anachronism, 8

T

television, 34, 41

U

units, how to join one, 15–16

V

Vietnam, 12, 16, 39–40

ABOUT THE AUTHOR

Monique Vescia is a writer who has always been fascinated by the past. Her doctoral dissertation examined connections between 1930s' documentary photography and modern American poetry, and she has written books about the history of food and fashion. Monique and her husband and teenage son visited Omaha Beach in Normandy, France, in 2014, on the seventieth anniversary of D-day. After studying so many grainy black-and-white images of that terrible WWII battle, she was astonished to find miles of golden sand and a peaceful blue ocean that seemed to go on forever.

PHOTO CREDITS